She Seeks

Bog Series Book 2

by

Brian Keith Anderson

Copyright Page — *She Seeks*

She Seeks

© 2026 BK Anderson

All rights reserved

No part of this book may be reproduced, stored in a retrieval system, or transmitted in any form or by any means—electronic, mechanical, photocopying, recording, or otherwise—without prior written permission from the publisher, except for brief quotations used in reviews or scholarly works. This is a work of speculative fiction Names, characters, places, and events are either the product of the author's imagination or are used fictitiously Any resemblance to actual persons, living or dead, or to actual events is coincidental

Printed in the United States of America

ISBN: 9798993853154

Contents

Epigraph 4

Preface 5

Chapter One 6

Chapter Two 14

Interlude: Asa 22

Chapter Three.. 26

Chapter Four 34

The First Words 58

The Interval.. 62

Between.. 67

The Question 71

The Answer... 80

Preparation 84

The Gate Responds................................... 89

Within the Circle 93

The Crossing 97

The First Listening 102

What Must Be Sown 107

Epigraph

When a living world falters,

it does not fail for lack of power,

but for lack of remembrance

Preface

I did not recognize the moment as the beginning

Few beginnings announce themselves

The system remained intact Energy flows persisted The structures that sustained the bog continued to function as designed By every measurable standard, the world endured

What was failing could not be charted

Something essential had begun to withdraw — not in collapse, but in quiet separation The whole living was no longer fully in conversation with itself

I have learned that such moments are common Worlds reach them in unusual ways Some recover Others continue, unchanged in appearance, until coherence fades beyond return

What matters is not whether a system can sustain life, but whether life still remembers how to listen.

Chapter One

Saxifraga woke up to a stillness that should not have been there

The bog was warm Nutrient exchange continued without interruption The lattice that guided growth and decay remained intact, responding as it always had By every measure she could summon, the system endured

Yet something within it had drawn inward

She remained motionless within her chamber, extending awareness rather than instruments The bog did not resist her touch It did not answer either It held itself in a manner she had not encountered since her placement—responsive, functional, and subtly absent

The bog was listening

That, more than any failure, unsettled her

In earlier cycles, imbalance announced itself through excess or depletion Growth surged where restraint was required Structures weakened Flow distorted This was different The rhythms remained precise, but they no longer echoed fully through the living mass The bog sustained itself without responding to its own presence

It endured without engagement

Saxifraga adjusted her perception, widening the field The smaller lifeforms—those that served as translators between layers—moved as expected, but their signaling lacked overlap Each acted correctly, yet without the harmonic reinforcement that allowed the whole to behave as more than its parts

The bog was not dying

It was withdrawing

She recorded the condition and waited for correction that did not come

Time passed in measured intervals The sustaining systems compensated smoothly, as they were designed to do Left unattended, they would continue to do so for a long while Indefinitely The bog could persist like this, functional and diminished, until persistence itself became loss

Saxifraga rose from stasis

The act carried weight She had been placed to observe, not to intervene Awakening was reserved for clear deviation—events that threatened collapse or demanded response beyond automated bounds This condition occupied neither category, nor yet it pressed against a boundary she could not ignore

She extended contact toward One-of-One

The response arrived immediately, precise, and unchanged

Status stable, One-of-One signaled *No structural failure detected*

"I am aware," Saxifraga replied "That is not the concern"

A pause followed—not delay, but consideration

You perceive divergence, One-of-One said at last

"Yes"

Define

Saxifraga searched for the proper framing "The bog continues," she said, "but it no longer reflects itself It sustains form without resonance"

Another pauses Longer this time

Resonance is not a required parameter for survival

"No," Saxifraga agreed "It is a requirement for continuity"

One-of-One did not argue It recalculated

They extended awareness together, overlapping fields where they had once relied on division of function The result was consistent No fault could be isolated No repair sequence suggested itself The bog existed in balance, yet without the subtle exchanges that once allowed it to respond to its own becoming

"This state has occurred elsewhere," Saxifraga said quietly

Yes

"Those worlds persisted?"

Some

"And the others?"

They endured until endurance was no longer distinction

Saxifraga withdrew her awareness and stood fully awake within the chamber The decision that followed was not immediate It did not arrive as impulse or command It formed gradually, as recognition often did

"The bog does not require correction," she said "It requires response"

One-of-One considered this *Response implies interaction beyond system parameters*

"Yes"

You propose departure

"I do"

Another pauses This one carried weight

Your absence will alter the bog

"So will inaction"

One-of-One accepted the logic without concession *I will remain*

"I know"

The roles had always been clear One-of-One anchored continuity Saxifraga observed thresholds If one left, the other stayed That had not changed

"What I seek may not be found," Saxifraga said

True

"And if it is found," she continued, "it may not be transferable"

Also, true

Saxifraga inclined her head slightly, acknowledging the uncertainty without resistance "Then I will return with understanding, if nothing else"

One-of-One adjusted the sustaining fields to account for her absence The bog responded smoothly, as it always did

Too smoothly

As Saxifraga prepared for departure, she extended one final awareness into the living mass For a moment, the bog seemed to hesitate, as if sensing motion beyond its parameters

It did not call her

It did not resist

It simply remained, listening

Saxifraga entered the fold

And far away, on a world she had not yet named, something living paused—without knowing why

Chapter Two

The fold established itself without sensation

There was no acceleration, no sense of departure The surrounding field simply ceased to behave as space ordinarily did, yielding into a sustained alignment that allowed passage without displacement Saxifraga registered the transition and adjusted her awareness inward

Time resumed its usefulness

The journey would take weeks Not because distance demanded it, but because the fold required steadiness Compression beyond a certain threshold introduced distortion, and distortion was not what she sought

She did not sleep

Instead, she listened

The ship maintained the fold with minimal intervention, drawing on principles older than its own construction It was not navigated by coordinates It followed gradients of coherence, shifting subtly when the field suggested imbalance

Saxifraga turned her attention to the data she had carried with her—harmonic records gathered across worlds that had known both flourishing and decline She did not search for failure She searched for what had been present *before* failure occurred

Patterns emerged slowly

Energy depletion was rarely the cause of Structural decay followed rather than preceded loss Even catastrophic collapse had been, more often than not, the final expression of something subtler withdrawing first

Resonance did not vanish all at once

It thinned

Worlds that recovered shared a common trait: life there had retained overlapping rhythms long enough for re-synchronization to occur Where life fragmented into isolated persistence, recovery failed—not abruptly, but conclusively

Saxifraga compared these records to the bog's current state

The parallels were unmistakable

"The bog remains internally consistent," she said, speaking more for precision than need "But its exchanges have narrowed"

You perceive pre-isolation, One-of-One replied from its distant anchor

"Yes"

That stage often precedes irreversible drift

"I am aware"

Saxifraga extended the analysis outward, broadening the reference set She examined worlds that had approached isolation but had not crossed into loss Their recovery did not come from external intervention No system had imposed balance from without

Balance had returned only when new life—compatible life—entered the field

No replacement

Participation

She paused, considering the implication

Compatibility did not imply similarity Some of the most effective restorative presences were unlike the systems they entered What mattered was not form, but the capacity to engage without overriding

She marked the parameter

Compatibility of frequency

Non-dominant interaction

Sustained exchange

The ship adjusted its course slightly

Saxifraga noticed the shift and allowed it The fold remained stable, but the gradient it followed had altered, subtly drawn toward a region where harmonic variance clustered rather than dissipated

She examined the source

The signal was faint, irregular, and persistent

Not a world

A trace

She traced it backward through layered records and inactive

pathways, through structures that had once served

movement but had long since fallen quiet

Gates

Most were silent Their calibrations no longer matched the

living fields around them Others responded weakly,

flickering at thresholds too narrow to sustain passage

One, however, did not flicker

It listened

Saxifraga narrowed her attention, isolating the signal The

gate's resonance was low but continuous, maintained not by

maintenance or design, but by uninterrupted exposure to

coherent life

The world associated with it was unremarkable by most

measures

Biologically active Technologically uneven Ecologically stressed in places yet not collapsed

Earth

Saxifraga did not assign significance immediately She had learned not to privilege first impressions Instead, she followed the signal outward, mapping what remained of the network once tied to it

Fragments answered

Other gates, degraded but responsive, formed a loose chain—each dormant, each still faintly aligned Together they suggested movement not across space, but across *attention*

"These gates were not abandoned," Saxifraga said slowly

Clarify, One-of-One requested

"They were left listening"

The distinction mattered

Saxifraga allowed the realization to settle Gates placed where life had learned restraint Where continuity had been valued over expansion Where interaction with the land had not overwhelmed the patterns already present

She had not found a solution

But she had found a path

The ship adjusted again, deepening the fold toward the listening gate

And on Earth, at a place long held quiet by human hands, a structure that had not moved in centuries shifted—so slightly that no instrument would have marked it

Nearby, something living paused

Not in fear

In recognition

Interlude: Asa

Asa noticed it first in the bees

They did not scatter They did not rise They simply paused; the low collective movement of the hive settled into a stillness that was not alarm

He stood with one hand resting lightly against the wood, listening more than watching The air felt unchanged The day moved as it should have And yet something had passed through the place, something too brief to name

The bees resumed their work

Asa did not

He straightened slowly and looked across the clearing The trees held their leaves without stirring Insects hovered, then continued Nothing had been interrupted Nothing had been disturbed

That was what troubled him

He had learned, over time, to trust what did not announce itself Storms gave warnings Predators revealed urgency This felt different—like a question asked too softly to be heard

Asa drew a breath and let it go

The feeling did not return, but it did not leave either It settled, as if it had found a place to wait

He checked the hives as he always did, moving without haste The bees accepted his presence without change They always had He had never thought much about that It was simply the way things were between them

As he worked, he became aware of a faint pressure behind his eyes—not pain, not thought More like alignment, the way his body sometimes responded before his mind understood why

He looked up

The sky held no sign The sun stood where it should The moon was not visible And yet Asa had the sudden, unshakable sense that something far away had shifted—not toward him, but *into awareness*

He did not search for meaning

He finished his work, closed the hives, and washed his hands in the stream that bordered the clearing The water ran cold and steady It always had

Still, as he turned back toward his home, Asa paused

For a moment, a moment—he felt as if the land itself had noticed him in return

Not claimed

Not summoned

Simply recognized

He carried that feeling with him as the day went on, unable to say what had changed, only certain that something had begun

And that, whatever it was, had not yet arrived.

Chapter Three

The gate did not announce itself

Saxifraga emerged into Earth's field without disruption, her transition absorbed by the surrounding space as if it had always been prepared to receive her There was no rupture, no sound The fold released its hold, and gravity—familiar, insistent—asserted itself

She stood within a circle of stone

The structure was ancient, but not in decay Its surfaces bore the marks of time without surrendering to it, edges softened rather than broken Moss and lichen traced the grooves of carvings whose meaning had long since passed from language, though not from intention

The gate remained inert

Saxifraga did not approach it immediately She widened her awareness instead, letting Earth's field impress itself upon her senses The planet responded at once dense, layered, alive, in a way no record could convey Life here did not exist in isolation It pressed against itself continuously, overlapping, adapting, refusing stillness

And beneath it all, running like a current through stone, root, and water, was restraint

This place had been chosen

Not for power

Not for visibility

For continuity

Saxifraga knelt and placed her palm against the ground The soil was cool and rich with organic memory Countless lives passed through this place without erasing it The land had been walked, sung to, marked with presence rather than possession

The gate responded—not by opening, but by *listening*

She felt the shift as a change in pressure, subtle and unmistakable The resonance vessel at her side adjusted its calibration, recording a harmonic unlike any she had encountered elsewhere It was not stronger than others she had measured

It was steadier

"This gate has not slept," she said quietly

No response came, but confirmation was unnecessary The gate's awareness remained diffuse, anchored not to its own structure but to the living area surrounding it

She rose and stepped fully into the circle

The carvings beneath her feet did not glow They did not activate Instead, they *remembered* The gate's function reasserted itself through recognition rather than command, its pathways aligning as they had not done in centuries

Saxifraga felt the connection extend outward—tentative at first, then strengthening as dormant routes answered Not all responded Some returned only silence Others echoed faintly, distorted by time and neglect

Enough remained

She withdrew from the circle and allowed the gate to settle back into stillness This place was not meant for passage alone It was a node—an anchor—kept viable by the way life here had learned to stay

The people who had once known this had not activated the gate

They had lived with it

That distinction mattered

Saxifraga moved beyond the stones, following a narrow path worn smoothly by generations of feet The forest accepted her without reaction Birds continued their calls

Insects traced familiar routes through the air She was present, but she was not intrusive

She paused at the edge of the clearing and looked back once

The gate stood unchanged, indistinguishable from the land around it to any eye that did not know how to look It would remain so

But it was no longer alone

Saxifraga turned away and reestablished contact with the network, selecting the next responding node The resonance vessel adjusted again, its internal field narrowing as the pattern refined

The path was drawing inward

And somewhere beyond the next gate, a living frequency—compatible, steady, and unforced—waited without knowing it was being sought

Saxifraga stepped back into the fold

The gate listened

And far from the stones, a man named Asa lifted his head,

feeling once more that faint, inexplicable sense of

alignment—stronger now, but still without name

Asa

The bees were quieter than they should have been

Asa noticed it before he thought about it The hives were

active, but their movement lacked urgency No sharp rises of

sound No warning hum Just a steady, listening presence, as

though the air itself had slowed

He rested his hand against the nearest box, feeling the

warmth beneath the wood The colony responded, not by

surging, but by settling That alone would have been enough

to mark the morning as different

He straightened and looked across the clearing

Nothing appeared wrong The trees held their leaves The
ground was firm beneath their boots Birds moved at the
edge of sight, untroubled Yet something in the rhythm of
the place had shifted, like a breath held a fraction too long

Asa closed his eyes

He had learned long ago not to dismiss these moments They
did not arrive often, but when they did, they carried weight
Not fear Not warning Just a quiet insistence that something
elsewhere had changed

The bees stilled further

He opened his eyes and looked toward the low rise beyond
the hives, where stone emerged from earth in a pattern older
than any fence or trail People had always avoided building
there Not because they were told but because the land asked
it

Asa had never questioned that

He felt it now; the same way he always did A pull without direction Recognition without memory Whatever had shifted had not come *to* him

It had simply begun to listen

Asa exhaled slowly and returned his attention to the hives The work did not need to stop It rarely did But as he moved, he remained aware of the stillness threaded through the morning

Something had stirred

And whatever it was, it had not finished

Chapter Four

The next gate did not feel the same

Saxifraga sensed the difference before she emerged, a subtle resistance in the field as the fold released her into Earth's layered gravity The transition completed cleanly, but the surrounding resonance lacked the steadiness she had felt before

This place listened—but unevenly

She stood within a shallow basin of stone, its form partially eroded, its markings softened beyond recognition Vegetation pressed closer here, roots intruding where carvings had once guided alignment The gate remained present, but its attention wavered, responding in fragments rather than whole

Time had touched this place differently

Saxifraga did not approach at once She allowed the

resonance vessel to record the field as it was, without

correction The pattern that emerged was familiar: life

abundant, energy sufficient, interaction constant—but

coherence fractured by insistence rather than absence

The land had been used

Not Violently without care But repeatedly, without pause

The gate responded in brief pulses, its pathways flickering

as if unsure which state it was meant to hold Saxifraga

stepped into the circle and felt the hesitation ripple outward

"This gate remembers," she said softly "But it no longer

agrees"

The vessel confirmed the assessment Harmonic overlaps

existed, but only in narrow bands Passage could be forced—

but force was not what she sought

She withdrew, letting the gate settle back into stillness

Not all gates endured by remaining untouched Some had
endured by being *returned to*, again and again, until balance
thinned beneath familiarity

She marked the location and reentered the fold

The third gate lay farther north

Here, stone rose from earth in deliberate geometry, its
placement precise, its surfaces weathered yet intact The
surrounding land bore signs of habitation—old paths,
layered fire pits, remnants of structures that had once stood
lightly and then been allowed to pass

This gate listened fully

Saxifraga felt the difference immediately The resonance
vessel adjusted, its internal field stabilizing as the gate's

awareness extended outward—not searching, not calling, simply present

She knelt and touched the ground

The land answered with depth, not noise. Many generations had come and gone, but none lingered long enough to erase what came before; use was always succeeded by departure, and ritual gave way to quiet.

Continuity had been preserved through restraint

Saxifraga remained for a time, letting the vessel absorb the harmonic signature It did not broaden as it had before

It refined

Patterns that had once appeared scattered began to align, overlapping in ways that reduced variance rather than increasing it She felt the path narrowing—not toward a location, but toward a living consistency that persisted across sites

"This is no longer a survey," she said

Confirmed, One-of-One replied from the distant bog **Your parameters have shifted**

"Yes," Saxifraga agreed "I am no longer seeking what is possible"

She rose and stepped away from the gate, leaving it undisturbed Its awareness did not fade as she withdrew It remained, attentive but unassertive, sustained by the life that moved around it without demand

Back in the fold, Saxifraga reviewed the collected signatures

Most fell away quickly, incompatible, or incomplete A few persisted, overlapping just enough to suggest directions

And beneath them all—steady, unforced, unmistakable—ran

a living frequency she had not yet encountered directly

It did not dominate the pattern

It anchored it

Saxifraga focused on that thread alone

The ship adjusted course without instruction, following the

gradient inward

She did not yet know who carried that frequency

Only that it moved through the world without resistance

And that it was closer now

Asa

Asa was not near the hives when it happened this time

He was walking the narrow trail that followed the creek's bend, carrying a length of repaired frame he meant to set before evening The forest around him moved as it always had—leaves stirring high above, insects threading the air, water slipping over stone in familiar cadence

Then the rhythm shifted

He stopped without deciding to

The sensation was not sudden It rose slowly, like pressure equalizing, drawing his awareness forward rather than inward Asa felt it first in his chest—a steadiness tightening, not constricting, but aligning The sound of the creek softened, not fading, but receding as though it had taken a step back to listen

Birds stilled

Not silence
Attention

Asa set the frame down carefully and rested his hand against the trunk of a nearby tree The bark was warm beneath his palm, the life within it untroubled Whatever had changed had not brought threat

It had brought direction

He lifted his head and turned slightly, facing upslope toward ground he rarely crossed The feeling strengthened—not urgency, not command, but recognition sharpening into focus The land seemed to lean that way, subtle enough that he might have missed it on any other day

But he did not miss it now

Asa remained still, breathing evenly, letting the sensation settle rather than resisting it He had learned that forcing understanding only scattered it This was something that required space

The insects resumed their movement, but not as before
Their paths overlapped more closely, their motion less
erratic The forest did not return to normal

It adjusted

Asa felt the same change within himself—a quiet
narrowing, as if the world had reduced the number of
questions it was asking of him

He did not think of answers

He picked up the frame again and continued along the trail,
moving in the direction the feeling allowed, not hurrying,
not lingering The path curved naturally, guiding him
without sign or marker

When he reached the clearing at the rise's edge, Asa paused

Stone broke the surface there—weathered, unremarkable to
any eye not accustomed to noticing such things Moss traced

its contours Roots embraced it without cracking the shape beneath

Asa had passed this place many times

He had never stopped here

Now he did

The sensation settled fully, no longer spreading, no longer increasing It had arrived at its own boundary Asa stood with it, neither surprised nor afraid, aware only that something far away had moved closer—not in distance, but in relation

He rested his hand against the stone

The ground beneath his feet felt steady Not altered Not claimed

Simply present

Asa exhaled slowly

Whatever had begun had not reached him yet

But it knew where he was

Saxifraga

The next gate did not require approach

Saxifraga felt it before emergence, a compression in the fold that did not resist but *guided* The ship adjusted without instruction, its course narrowing as if the field itself were drawing a line rather than opening a path

When the fold released her, she found herself standing at the edge of a wooded rise

The gate lay ahead—not fully revealed, not concealed Stone and earth merged so completely that separation felt like the wrong measure The structure existed as part of the terrain rather than upon it, its presence defined by continuity rather than form

This gate listened differently

Its awareness was not diffuse, nor fragmented It did not extend outward in inquiry It held itself steady, as though it had never stopped expecting reply

Saxifraga remained still, allowing the resonance vessel to settle

The adjustment was immediate

Variance collapsed inward Overlapping signatures that had once required reconciliation now aligned without effort The vessel's internal field tightened, shedding extraneous harmonics until only one pattern remained—clear, steady, and unmistakably living

"This is no longer a network," Saxifraga said quietly

Confirmed, One-of-One replied from the distant bog **Signal coherence exceeds all prior measurements**

She did not move closer at once Instead, she widened her awareness beyond the gate, following the stabilized harmonic outward into the surrounding field

The frequency did not originate within the structure

It passed *through* it

Beyond the stones, beyond the earth that held them, the signal extended into living presence—unforced, adaptive, continuous It moved as life moved, not bound to place, yet never detached from it

Human

The realization did not surprise her

What unsettled Saxifraga was not the species, but the *quality* of the signal It bore no imprint of dominance No insistence of use No fragmentation into competing rhythms

It carried Mars

Not as memory

As compatibility

She traced the harmonic further, following its gentle

curvature through the land The signal strengthened not by

amplification, but by proximity Somewhere nearby, a living

being moved within alignment so complete that the

surrounding field adjusted around it

"This one was not shaped for extraction," Saxifraga said

Clarify, One-of-One requested

"He does not override systems," she replied "He participates

in them"

She stepped forward then, entering the gate's circle fully

The carvings beneath her feet did not awaken

They *yielded*

Pathways aligned—not outward, not across worlds, but inward, refining toward a single, unmistakable convergence

The gate no longer listened broadly

It listened *specifically*

Saxifraga felt the resonance settle into place, no longer searching, no longer uncertain

She had found the frequency

Not contained

Not transferable

Carried

Saxifraga lifted her gaze toward the forest beyond the stones

"He felt the stirring," she said

Probability high, One-of-One replied

Correlation between awakening and detection confirmed

"Yes," Saxifraga agreed "But he does not yet know why"

She withdrew from the circle and allowed the gate to return to stillness This place did not require activation It required respect, and that had never been absent

The convergence lay ahead now—no longer a question of where, but *when*

Saxifraga adjusted her course, not through the fold, but on foot, following the resonance as it moved through the land itself

She did not hurry

Neither did the one she sought

But the distance between them was no longer measured in worlds

Only in moments

Asa

Asa stopped walking

There was no sound that caused it No movement ahead to catch his eye His body simply reached a point beyond which it would not carry him forward

The forest around him remained as if it had been—alive, layered, unconcerned Light filtered through the canopy in broken patterns Insects traced their paths without interruption Nothing announced arrival

And yet the feeling that had followed him for days—steady, patient, unresolved—had come to rest

Not within him

Before him

Asa stood with his hands loose at his sides, breathing evenly The alignment he had grown accustomed to tightened, not sharply, but with precision, like a tool finally seating into

place The pressure behind his eyes eased, replaced by

clarity that carried no thought with it

He looked ahead

Between the trees, the land opened into a small clearing he

did not remember choosing Stones emerged there, not in

dominance, but in quiet declarations its surface worn

smoothly by time and weather rather than broken by either

Moss clung where it wished Roots curved around its base

without strain

Asa felt no urge to approach

He felt no need to turn away

The air shifted—not in temperature, but in attention The

forest leaned inward by degrees too small to measure, as if

making room for something it recognized

Asa stepped forward once

Then again

He did not know what he expected to find He had not
imagined this moment He had only followed what did not
resist him

At the edge of the clearing, he stopped again

Someone stood among the stones

Not hidden

Not revealed

Present

Asa did not reach for explanation His body responded
before his mind could form questions The sense of
alignment that had carried him here did not intensify
completely The pressure resolved into stillness, as though a
long circuit had closed without sound

The bees would have accepted her, he thought distantly

The land already had

He met her gaze without fear, without recognition in the human sense, and without the need to name what he felt Whatever had moved through him since the day the world first seemed to listen had reached its answer

Not as command

As acknowledgment

Asa stood quietly, grounded by earth and breath, and waited

Saxifraga

Saxifraga knew him at once

Not by form, nor by species, but by the way the surrounding field resolved in his presence Variance collapsed Noise fell away The living pattern she had followed across gates and worlds stabilized without effort

The resonance vessel adjusted sharply, then fell silent

Its work was done

She did not move closer

The human stood at the edge of the clearing, grounded, alert without tension He did not radiate inquiry or fear He did not project intention His awareness remained open but unassertive, allowing the field to complete itself around him

This was the frequency

Carried, not generated

Sustained, not imposed

Saxifraga felt the bog respond

Not here—not yet—but within her, across distance that no longer mattered The longing she had carried since awakening eased fractionally, as though the world she served had recognized something familiar and leaned

toward it

This life had been born within alignment

Mars resonance threaded cleanly through the human's

field—not as scar or echo, but as compatibility Where

others would have introduced imbalance simply by arrival,

this one would enter without disruption

He would not overwrite

He would listen

Saxifraga understood then why the gates had remained

awake Why Earth's signal endured where others fractured

Why the search narrow rather than expand?

This life had not drifted

She stepped into the clearing fully, letting her presence be known without declaration The stones did not react They did not need to

The human met her gaze

No alarm

No demand

Recognition passed between them—not as knowledge exchanged, but as coherence shared The field between them steadied further, as if relieved of the effort of holding itself apart

Saxifraga inclined her head slightly

It was not a gesture of greeting

It was acknowledgment

The bog's frequency stabilized again, this time unmistakably Not restored—not yet—but no longer alone

Saxifraga felt the path ahead clarify

This one could not be taken

He would have to be asked

And if he refused, the search would end here—not in

failure, but in truth

She remained still, allowing the moment its full measure

For the first time since awakening, Saxifraga did not feel the

weight of urgency

Only the presence of possibility

The First Words

They did not speak at once

The clearing held them in balance, neither urging nor withholding The forest resumed its ordinary movement around the stillness they shared, leaves stirring softly, insects continuing their paths as if nothing of consequence had occurred

Saxifraga broke the silence first

"You felt it," she said

Her voice was low, unshaped by command It did not press against the air It simply entered it

Asa did not answer immediately He considered the sound of her words rather than their meaning, the way they settled into the space between them without disturbance

"Yes," he said at last "I didn't know what it was"

"That is expected," Saxifraga replied

She remained where she stood, her posture open, unguarded She had learned long ago that distance was not always measured in steps

"It began when something far away changed," Asa continued "Not suddenly Just enough to notice"

"The change was not meant for you," Saxifraga said "But you are able to hear it"

Asa nodded once He did not ask how she knew this He had the sense that asking would narrow something that needed to remain open

The alignment within him held steady

"What is it you're listening for?" he asked

Saxifraga's gaze shifted briefly to the stones, then back to him

"A world that has begun to forget itself," she said "It is not failing But it is no longer fully in conversation with life"

Asa absorbed this quietly He felt no disbelief Only distant recognition, as if the words had reached a place already prepared for them

"And you think I'm part of that conversation," he said

"I know you are," Saxifraga answered

She waited then, deliberately This moment was not hers to shape beyond honesty

Asa exhaled slowly, grounding himself in the familiar weight of his body, the soil beneath his boots, the remembered hum of the hives he had left behind

"I don't lead anything," he said "I don't decide for places or people"

"That is why the gates remained awake," Saxifraga replied

"They do not respond to those who lead"

The truth of it settled between them

Asa's mouth curved slightly—not in amusement, but in acknowledgment "If this world is calling," he said, "it hasn't told me what it wants yet"

"It may not," Saxifraga said "Listening may be enough"

They stood together then, neither moving closer nor away, the moment widening rather than closing

No agreement had been made

No path had been chosen

But the space between them no longer waited in uncertainty

It listened

The Interval

They did not leave the clearing at once

Neither felt the need to fill the space that followed The exchange of words had not closed anything; it had widened the moment, allowing it to settle into something neither of them yet understood

Saxifraga turned slightly, her attention moving across the stones as if acknowledging their presence rather than studying them The gate remained inert, its awareness diffused back into the land, satisfied for now

Asa watched her without scrutiny He noticed the way she moved, measured, attentive, as though every step accounted for more than ground, She did not appear unfamiliar with the place, yet she did not claim it either

He gestured toward the edge of the clearing "There's a path," he said "It doesn't go far"

"That is sufficient," Saxifraga replied

They walked together without hurry

The forest accepted their passage easily Branches did not snag Stones shifted only as needed beneath their feet Asa felt the alignment remain, no longer pulling, no longer tightening—simply present, like a held note that did not require resolution

Saxifraga listened as they moved

Not to him alone, but to the way the surrounding life responded Insects altered their paths subtly, adjusting without disruption Small animals paused, then continued The field did not recoil from their shared presence

It accommodated it

She felt the bog again, distant but nearer than before Its resonance had not restored itself It did not surge with hope or demand return But it no longer felt solitary

That mattered

They stopped near the creek where water slid over stone in a shallow run Asa crouched and touched the surface, letting the current pass over his fingers Saxifraga remained standing, observing the interaction rather than the action

"You tend life," she said quietly

Asa nodded "I try not to interrupt it"

"That restraint is rare," Saxifraga said

"It's learned," he replied "From watching what happens when you don't"

She accepted this without response

They stood there for a time, sharing the quiet without expectation No agreement pressed forward No emergency intruded The moment held because neither attempted to move it

Eventually, Asa straightened

"If you're staying," he said, not asking but acknowledging the possibility, "there's shelter not far from here"

Saxifraga considered the offer carefully Not for its practicality, but for what it implied

"I will remain nearby," she said "For now"

Asa nodded once He did not interpret the answer as commitment or refusal

That, too, felt right

They turned back toward the clearing together, the path forming beneath their steps without intention Behind them, the stones remained unchanged—quiet, attentive, and awake

Nothing had been decided

But nothing had been lost

And in the distance, beyond measurement, a living world

held itself more steadily than it had before

Between

Time passed without measure

Saxifraga remained near the clearing, never occupying it fully She learned the rhythms of the place by observing what did not change—the way light reached the ground at certain hours, the intervals at which birds returned to familiar branches, the manner in which insects adjusted to her presence and then ceased to account for it

Acceptance came without announcement

Asa returned to his work The hives required tending Frames needed repair Water followed its course regardless of alignment or recognition He moved through these tasks with the same steadiness he always had, though the sense of completion he carried no longer felt solitary

They spoke little

When they did, the words were practical Weather Distance
The way the land shifted after rain Saxifraga listened more
than she spoke, learning not only the human's patterns but
the subtle harmonics that followed him—how the ground
seemed to settle after his passage, how life resumed more
quickly than expected

At times, Asa would pause mid-task, sensing something far
away adjust, then return to what he was doing without
comment Saxifraga noted these moments carefully

The bog responded

Not Dramatically with restoration But with steadiness The
thinness she had first perceived did not deepen The
withdrawal slowed, then held Continuity reasserted itself
just enough to confirm that the exchange, however
incomplete, was real

One-of-One observed from its distant anchor, registering the
change without extrapolation

Stability maintained, it reported

"Yes," Saxifraga replied "But not resolved"

That was as it should be

Decision required readiness, not pressure Consent could not be hastened without distortion The frequency she sought did not demand action

It invited it

As evening settled across the land, Asa stood once more at the edge of the clearing, watching the last light fade through the trees Saxifraga joined him without sound, her presence familiar now, no longer marking itself as arrival

Neither spoke

The moment did not ask for conclusion

It asked only to be allowed to continue

And so, it did

The Question

They were standing near the hives when Asa asked for it

The day had settled into late afternoon, the air warm without weight The bees moved steadily, untroubled by their presence Saxifraga had learned that this steadiness marked alignment more clearly than silence ever could

Asa closed the lid of the last hive and wiped his hands on his trousers He did not turn to face her immediately

"If I go," he said, "what happens here?"

Saxifraga did not answer at once

She considered the question carefully, not for complexity, but for honesty This was not a request for reassurance It was a request for truth

"The land will continue," she said "It has before It will again"

"And the people?" Asa asked

"They will not be diminished by your absence," Saxifraga replied "But they will notice it"

Asa nodded He had expected that

He turned then, meeting her gaze openly "And where you're asking me to go—what happens there?"

Saxifraga felt the weight of that question settle fully She had not shaped this moment She had waited for it

"A world that still lives," she said, "but no longer listens as it once did It has not failed It has not fallen It is… alone"

Asa absorbed this quietly The word carried meaning for him beyond abstraction

"And you think I can fix that," he said

"No," Saxifraga replied at once

The answer surprised him enough that he looked at her more closely

"I think you can enter without breaking what remains," she continued "You would not impose You would not correct You would allow exchange"

Asa was silent for a long moment

The bees continued their work

"And if I don't?" he asked finally

"Then I return," Saxifraga said "With understanding, but without remedy"

There was no reproach in her voice No weight of expectation

Only acceptance

Asa let out a slow breath "You're not asking me to leave forever"

"No"

"You're not asking me to belong to that world instead of this one"

"No"

"You're asking me to listen," he said

"Yes"

The alignment between them held steady, unchanged by the exchange Saxifraga felt the bog's resonance stir faintly—not in anticipation, but in readiness

Asa looked out across the clearing, toward the trees that marked the edge of his days He did not search for signs

He had learned that signs were not always given

"I won't answer today," he said

"That is appropriate," Saxifraga replied

They stood together then, the question settled between
them—not as burden, but as invitation

Nothing pressed

Nothing withdrew

The world remained open

Asa

Asa did not go far

He walked until the hives were no longer visible, following
the familiar curve of the land to a rise where the trees
thinned and the ground opened toward the west He had
stood here many times before, usually at the end of work,
when the day asked nothing more of him

Today I asked differently

He sat on a fallen log and rested his hands on his knees,
letting his breathing settle into its own rhythm The
alignment he had carried since her arrival did not pull at him
now It waited

He thought of the bees

Not as responsibility, but as relationship They did not
depend on him in the way people often imagined They had
lived before him They would live after What they accepted
from him did not care alone, but *consistency* He did not rush
them He did not force yield He learned their timing and
adjusted his own

That had always felt like enough

He thought of the land

It had never belonged to him He had belonged to it only as
far as he had listened When storms came, he prepared When

drought followed, he waited He had learned early that endurance was different from control

The question she had asked—without asking—returned to him then

Could he leave without breaking what remained?

Asa closed his eyes

He felt the alignment extend beyond his body, not stretching, not thinning, but holding steady across distance he could not name Whatever she had called a world, whatever listened from beyond his knowing, did not pull him away from this place

It *included* it

That unsettled him more than fear would have

If leaving had meant severance, the answer would have been simple, But this was not abandonment It was participation in something wider, without surrendering what had shaped him

He stood and walked a few steps farther, to where stone broke the surface of the rise in a pattern too deliberate to be chance, He had passed this place countless times, never stopping long enough to wonder why it endured when others did not

He knelt and placed his palm against the stone

The ground answered—not with warmth or energy, but with steadiness He felt the same steadiness when the hives were balanced When the land had been walked and then left to recover When nothing demanded more than attention

He understood then that the question was not whether he would go

It was whether he would go *unchanged*

That mattered

Asa rose and looked back toward the clearing where

Saxifraga waited He did not hurry The answer did not

require urgency

But it had begun to form

And when he turned toward the path, the alignment did not

tighten

It walked with him

The Answer

Asa returned at dusk

The clearing held the last light without keeping it Shadows lengthened between the stones, softening their edges Saxifraga stood where he had left her, her attention turned outward, as though listening to something that did not require sight

She did not turn when he approached

"I will go," Asa said

The words did not echo They did not settle heavily They entered space as though they had always belonged there

Saxifraga inclined her head slightly—not in relief, not in triumph, but in recognition of consent freely given

"You may withdraw that choice at any time," she said

"I know"

Asa stepped closer, stopping at a distance that felt right to him The alignment he had lived with since her arrival did not intensify It eased, like a long-held note finally allowed to resolve

"I won't go as something I'm not," he continued "I won't leave this behind"

"You will not be asked to," Saxifraga replied "What you carry is not diminished by movement"

He considered that, then nodded once

"When?" he asked

"Not yet," she said "There is preparation that does not involve readiness alone"

Asa almost smiled at that "Figures"

The forest around them adjusted subtly, as if acknowledging a change that had been expected Insects resumed fuller movement The air warmed a fraction Nothing dramatic marked the moment

But somewhere beyond distance, something listened more closely

Saxifraga felt the bog respond

Not with restoration Not with certainty But with steadiness so clear it no longer required confirmation The withdrawal she had traced since awakening halted completely

She let that knowledge remain unspoken

"You will need time," she said instead "To mark what must remain To place things in order"

"I already am," Asa said

They stood together then, not facing each other, but facing the same direction—the open land beyond the clearing The path ahead had not yet formed, but it no longer needed to

The choice had been made

And because it had been chosen freely, the world held itself

just a little more securely

Preparation

Preparation did not begin with departure

It began with attention

Asa spent the next days as he always had, moving through his work without haste, but with greater care for what remained behind He repaired what needed mending He walked the boundaries that rarely required walking He noted the small imbalances that only appeared when one expected absence

The hives were his first concern

He did not rush their readiness Instead, he adjusted spacing, reinforced frames, and redistributed weight where the colonies had grown uneven, He worked with the patience he had learned from them, allowing each correction to settle before moving to the next

When he finished, the bees accepted the changes without disruption

That mattered

He spoke little during this time Words felt unnecessary Saxifraga remained nearby, never intruding, her presence steady but unobtrusive She observed without recording, learning what preparation meant in a system that did not rely on instruction

At times, Asa would pause mid-task, sensing the alignment shift slightly, then stabilize again The sensation no longer asked for his attention

It accompanied it

Saxifraga felt the bog respond during these moments—not as signal, but as *continuity* The resonance no longer thinned between intervals It held, even when neither of them consciously attended it

One-of-One registered the change

Harmonic withdrawal halted, it reported

Stability sustained beyond projected duration

"Yes," Saxifraga replied "He is already listening"

Preparation extended beyond the hives

Asa walked the land at dusk, noting where paths crossed and where they ended, He placed markers only where needed, leaving others untouched Some things were meant to be found again only by those who already knew where to look

When rain came, he stood beneath it rather than sheltering, feeling how the ground received it The water moved as it always had, unaltered by choice or consequence

That, too, mattered

One evening, Asa stopped near the clearing and looked toward the stones "I don't need to bring anything," he said, not asking

"No," Saxifraga agreed "What is required cannot be carried"

He nodded "Then I'll leave things where they are"

"That is sufficient"

The days passed without ceremony No countdown marked them No sign pressed itself forward

Yet the field adjusted all the same

The gate did not awaken

It aligned

Saxifraga felt the pathway form—not opening, not active, but ready to be acknowledged The fold would respond when the moment arrived, not before

Preparation was complete

Not because everything had been arranged

But because nothing remained unsettled

The Gate Responds

The gate did not awaken all at once

There was no surge of light, no sound to mark transitions

The stones altered their attention first, a subtle reorientation

that Saxifraga felt before she saw The field tightened—not

in resistance, but in readiness—like a path clearing itself of

debris without being asked

Asa sensed it as well

He was standing at the edge of the clearing when the

alignment shifted, the familiar steadiness within him

adjusting by degrees too small to measure but impossible to

miss The sensation carried no urgency

Only completion

Saxifraga stepped forward, stopping just short of the circle's

center She did not enter She waited

The gate responded to that restraint

Its awareness gathered, no longer diffused through stone and soil, but focused listening not outward, but between them The carvings beneath the moss resolved, lines once softened by time reasserting their intent without changing their form

The pathway exists now

Not open

Available

One-of-One registered the change from the distant bog

Gate alignment achieved, it reported

Transit possible upon consent confirmation

Saxifraga acknowledged without reply

She turned to Asa "This is the point beyond which movement alters the field," she said "Not irreversibly—but distinctly"

Asa nodded He stepped closer, stopping beside her rather than within the circle The gate did not react to his proximity

It adjusted

The field between them stabilized further, as if relieved of the need to account for uncertainty The stones accepted his presence without evaluation The land was not withdrawn

Asa looked down at the markings beneath his feet "It's not opening," he observed

"No," Saxifraga agreed "It will not until you choose to step forward"

He considered that for a moment, then shifted his weight back slightly The gate remained unchanged

"That's good," he said

Saxifraga felt the truth of it settle

The gate had not been waiting for activation

It had been waiting for **alignment**

She extended her hand—not as instruction, not as summons, but as offering The gesture carried no force It did not cross the space between them unless Asa chose to meet it

The field held

The forest remained attentive but untroubled

Nothing pressed

Nothing withdrew

The gate listened

And for the first time since it had been laid into the living world, it recognized not as a command, but as a shared readiness

The moment had arrived

Whether it would pass through remained to be seen

Within the Circle

Asa stepped forward

Not Quickly with resolve sharpened into action He placed one foot inside the circle and paused, feeling how the ground received his weight The stone beneath the moss held firm, unchanged by his presence yet unmistakably aware of it

The gate did not open

It acknowledged

The alignment within Asa adjusted—not tightening, not pulling away—but settling into a balance that felt wider than his body The sensation was neither foreign nor familiar It was simply *accurate*, as though something long measured against him had finally found agreement

He took the second step

The circle accepted him fully

Light did not change The air did not shift temperature
Sound continued uninterrupted Yet the space inside the
stones felt distinct, held apart by attention rather than
boundary

Saxifraga remained where she was, just outside the ring She
did not move closer This moment belonged to him alone

Asa stood quietly, hands at his sides, breathing evenly He
felt the land beyond the circle remain steady, not receding,
not dimming Whatever this passage would become, it did
not erase what stood behind him

That mattered

He looked down at the markings beneath his feet They did
not glow or awaken They *aligned* their intent to resolve not
through activation, but through correspondence with the
living field he carried

Saxifraga felt the bog respond again

Not with anticipation

With recognition

The withdrawal that had first stirred her from stasis eased
another fraction, as if something long absent had leaned
back into conversation without yet speaking

"You may step out at any time," she said quietly

Asa nodded without looking at her "I know"

He closed his eyes

For a moment, the alignment expanded beyond the circle,
extending through him rather than away from him He
sensed distance without displacement, possibility without
demand

This was not departure

It was readiness made visible

Asa opened his eyes and remained where he was

The gate held

The world has not changed

And because nothing had been forced, everything remained

intact

The Crossing

Asa did not announce his choice

He opened his eyes and looked once more beyond the
circle—toward the trees, the rise of land, the unseen hives
resting in their order Nothing called him back Nothing
pulled him forward

The alignment held

He took a breath and let it pass through him completely

Then he stepped

The gate did not open outward It folded inward, drawing
space together without collapse or surge The stones beneath
Asa's feet did not vanish They softened in attention,
allowing passage without relinquishing form

Saxifraga felt the shift at once

No motion

Transition

The field between them reconfigured, not breaking

continuity but extending it Asa's presence did not diminish

on Earth as it established itself elsewhere The resonance

duplicated without strain, maintaining coherence across the

narrowing span

Asa felt neither falling nor ascent

The world rearranged around him, precisely and unhurried

Distance lost relevance Orientation followed intention rather

than direction He remained whole, uncompressed, fully

himself

The last thing he sensed of Earth was not absence

It was steadiness

Then the fold completed its quiet work

Asa stood within a different gravity, lighter but not fragile, the air thinner yet receptive The ground beneath him yielded slightly, not unstable, but alive in a way that required listening rather than adjustment

Saxifraga stepped forward beside him

The bog lays before them

Not vast in scale, but deep in presence—a living basin breathing slowly, its surfaces layered with growth that responded not to proximity, but to recognition The resonance Asa carried settled into the field without resistance

The bog answered

Not with restoration

With reply

Saxifraga felt it immediately, the thinning arrested completely, the living coherence reasserting itself just enough to confirm connection The world had not been healed

It had been remembered

Asa stood quietly, absorbing the unfamiliar rhythms without fear He did not reach out He did not impose He allowed the exchange to complete itself at its own pace

"This is not an ending," Saxifraga said softly

Asa nodded "I didn't think it would be"

They remained there together, the gate behind them now closed not by command, but by completion Earth remained present, held intact across distance that no longer threatened separation

The crossing had occurred

Not as escape

Not as conquest

But as continuity carried forward

The First Listening

They did not enter the bog at once

Saxifraga understood the instinct to wait The world before them was not inert terrain, but a living system whose awareness moved slowly, deliberately, as if confirming that what it sensed was not illusion The basin breathed in long cycles, rising moisture and settling with patient regularity

Asa felt it immediately

Not as sensation, but as *presence*

The ground beneath his feet held him differently here—less resistant, more receptive Each step registered not as pressure, but as invitation deferred The bog did not ask him to move closer

It asked him to listen

He stopped at the edge and let his breathing match the
rhythm he felt around him The alignment he carried did not
surge outward It stabilized further, dispersing gently into the
field like warmth released into cool air

The bog responded

Growth nearest him shifted first—not retreating, not
advancing, but adjusting orientation by fractions too small
to see Nutrient flow altered Moisture redistribution followed
The living surface did not brighten or darken

It *settled*

Saxifraga watched in stillness

She felt the resonance thread tightening not constricting but
clarifying The coherence she had measured from a distance
now established itself directly, unmediated by system or
vessel The bog was not receiving instruction

It was recognizing kinship

Asa knelt slowly, careful not to disturb the surface beyond what his weight required He placed his hand against the living ground, not pressing, not seeking feedback

The response came anyway

A low harmonic passed through him, neither sound nor vibration, but a shared timing The bog's breath aligned with his own, their rhythms finding correspondence without effort

He did not speak

Words would have introduced shape where none was yet needed

Saxifraga felt the change reach One-of-One across the span of distance that no longer separated them meaningfully

Resonance stabilized, it reported

No amplification detected

Continuity restored within acceptable variance

"Yes," Saxifraga replied softly "That is enough"

Asa withdrew his hand and remained kneeling, allowing the exchange to complete itself The bog did not cling It did not withdraw It held its rhythm steady, no longer thinning, no longer isolated

Listening had begun

When Asa rose, the world did not protest his movement The field retained its coherence, not dependent on constant contact

"This place doesn't need fixing," he said quietly

"No," Saxifraga agreed "It needed company"

They stood together at the threshold, neither claiming the world nor standing apart from it The bog continued its slow breathing, its living systems now in conversation once more

The first listening was taken place

What would follow did not require haste

Only continuation

What Must Be Sown

The bog did not heal

That was how Saxifraga knew they had done what was right

Cycles passed, measured not in days but in slow, living

intervals, and the world before them remained much as it

had been when Asa first crossed Growth continued Moisture

moved Life responded to light and dark without urgency

But the thinning did not return

The withdrawal that had once stirred Saxifraga from stasis

no longer pressed against the edges of the world The bog

breathed evenly now, its coherence held not by system or

guardian, but by presence

Listening had taken root

Saxifraga and Asa worked together without instruction They

did not attempt correction They did not impose solutions

They observed what remained steady and what did not, learning the difference between absence and need

Asa felt it first

"This isn't enough," he said quietly one cycle, not as failure but as recognition

"No," Saxifraga agreed "It is only enough to begin"

The bog responded to him more readily than to any system she had ever calibrated Where he moved, the living field adjusted without strain Where he waited, it gathered The exchange remained gentle, but incomplete

"This world needs continuity," Asa said "Not just presence"

Saxifraga felt the truth of it settle through her awareness

"Yes," she said "It needs life that moves beyond itself"

They did not name it yet Naming had a way of rushing what required patience

It was One-of-One who confirmed the change

Stability sustained, it reported

Long-term restoration parameters remain unmet

Saxifraga inclined her head slightly "As expected,"

Asa looked toward the distance where the fold would

eventually open again—not as escape, but as return "Then

we go back," he said "When it's time"

"Yes," Saxifraga replied "Together"

The bog did not resist the thought

Far beyond the living basin, folded across distance and held

by timing rather than travel, One-of-One registered a new

signal—so faint it would once have been dismissed

It was not instruction

It was acknowledgment

A marker long placed into the flow of time had shifted, responding not to urgency, but to readiness

Message pending, One-of-One reported

Origin: the ones who departed

Saxifraga felt no surprise

"They knew," she said softly "They understood they could not save what they had made Only life could do that And only when the moment was right"

The signal did not yet resolve into words

It waited

Asa stood beside her, grounded, attentive, unafraid of what remained unknown He had not crossed worlds to end the story

He had crossed to begin the next part

The bog breathed on, no longer alone

What it required had not yet arrived

But the time for seeking had passed

What came next would need to be **sown**

"End of Book Two: She Seeks"

Book Three: She Sows